THE BOXCAR CHILDREN®

CREATED BY
GERTRUDE CHANDLER WARNER

BOOK

149

THE DAY OF THE DEAD MYSTERY

ILLUSTRATED BY
ANTHONY VanARSDALE

ALBERT WHITMAN & COMPANY
CHICAGO, ILLINOIS

THE BOXCAR CHILDREN MYSTERIES

Contents

Two Celebrations

"Come on, you two!" Jessie Alden called to Violet and Benny. It was the evening of October 31: Halloween. The streetlights were just starting to come on, and trick-or-treating was about to begin.

Jessie didn't want her younger sister and brother to miss out on the fun. Henry, the oldest of the Alden children, stood with Jessie and Grandfather on the front porch. Their dog, Watch, waited patiently at their feet, his chin resting on his paws. Now that Henry was fourteen and Jessie was twelve, they had decided they were too old to dress up for Halloween, but they were excited to see the costumes Violet and Benny had been working on.

"Almost ready," Violet called from the front hall. "Making a last-minute change to a sesame seed!"

Henry and Jessie looked at each other in confusion, and Grandfather laughed.

"This surprise is going to be well worth the wait," Grandfather said. A moment later, Violet burst onto the porch.

"Voilà!" she cried. Ten-year-old Violet wore a black wig adorned with flowers and a colorful dress with a band of white lace running along the hem. She had long, dark eyebrows and held a paintbrush in her hand.

"Wow, Violet—you're an artist!" Henry said. Watch sat up and barked his approval.

"Not just any artist. Right, Violet?" Grandfather said with a knowing smile.

"That's right," Violet said. "I am dressed as Frida Kahlo, one of Mexico's great painters."

"I remember learning about her in art class," Jessie said. "She was famous for painting self-portraits. You look just like her, Violet! But...what does this have to do with a sesame seed?"

Violet laughed. "That wasn't for me—it was for

Benny. Speaking of which..." Violet cleared her throat. "Ahem. We're ready for the, uh, the main course!"

Benny stepped outside. He was moving a little more slowly than Violet had. For one thing, he was only six years old. For another, he was wearing a giant, round costume stuffed with newspaper.

"Benny, you're a cheeseburger!" Jessie said.

"A deluxe one too," Henry added, as he noticed all the ingredients Benny's costume included. There was a brown bun strapped to his front and back, then a layer of meat made from brown felt, a slice of yellow paper cheese, a red satin tomato, and a layer of ketchup made from ribbon. Benny, who wore a green hat, appeared to be the pickle. White circles of paper were taped to the front of the bun to look like sesame seeds.

"You know what they say," Benny said. "You are what you eat!"

Grandfather laughed. "Well done, you two!" He asked the children to stand together on the front steps with Watch and snapped a picture of them. "This is going to make a great memory someday. Now, you had better get going before it gets any later!"

The Aldens started down the street to the house of Violet and Benny's new friends, Gloria and Mateo Hidalgo. The children planned to trick-or-treat together. When they arrived at the Hidalgo house, a cozy stone cottage with a heavy oak front door, Benny tried to ring the doorbell. He couldn't quite reach because of his costume, so Jessie gave him a boost.

Mateo, who was seven, answered the door. Normally, Mateo was a quiet boy with straight, dark hair and glasses, but tonight he wore a spiky red wig and glitter around his eyes. A guitar hung over his shoulder.

"You're a rock star!" Benny said.

Mateo smiled shyly and nodded. "And wait until you see Gloria."

The kids stepped into the Hidalgos' living room just as Gloria was coming out of the kitchen. Violet knew from school that Gloria had an energetic personality and a joyful laugh. So it was a surprise to see her wearing a very serious face and a judge's black robe, with her long, straight hair pulled into a tight bun.

"Order in the court!" she said when she saw the Aldens. She held up her gavel. The children all laughed. It was fun that on Halloween you could pretend to be someone so different from yourself.

Mrs. Hidalgo followed her daughter out of the kitchen. She had the same dark eyes as Gloria, but she was taller and had a little gray hair. She wore bright red earrings and an apron with a dusting of flour on the front.

"Kids, you look fantastic!" Mrs. Hidalgo said.

"Are the trick-or-treaters here?" asked a voice coming from the den. Mr. Hidalgo soon emerged and joined them in the living room. The house was full of striking and colorful artwork, and he was making his way around to each painting and whisking it with a feather duster. As soon as he saw Benny, he clapped his hands. "Now that's a great costume," Mr. Hidalgo said to his wife.

Mrs. Hidalgo nodded. "And I love Violet's too," she said. "Frida Kahlo has always been an inspiration to me. I studied her work in art school."

She leaned down and kissed each of her children on the head. "Now, I expect you two to bring me lots of chocolate bars."

Mateo smiled. "We will, Mamá."

"Won't you be able to join us for trick-or-treating?" Henry asked.

"We wish we could, Henry," said Mrs. Hidalgo. "But we have a lot to do at home."

"It's only two days until Day of the Dead," Mr. Hidalgo explained.

Benny's eyes got big. "What's that?" he asked.

"Day of the Dead, or *Día de Muertos* in Spanish, isn't anything to be afraid of, Benny," said Gloria. "It's a day of celebration in Mexico—a time to honor our ancestors."

"Wow, that sounds important," Violet said. She loved learning about history and hearing stories of the past. She turned to Mrs. Hidalgo. "Are you baking something for the celebration?"

Mrs. Hidalgo nodded. "Yes, the *pan de muerto*— the bread of the dead. I'm mixing up the dough today and will bake it tomorrow so that it's ready in time."

"And I am cleaning the house," Mr. Hidalgo said. He pointed to the vacuum cleaner in the corner. "We want everything to be perfect as we welcome the spirits for their visit."

Jessie noticed that Benny was looking a little nervous with all the talk of spirits. She cleared her throat and asked as politely as she could, "Mrs. Hidalgo, why is it called the bread of the dead?"

Mrs. Hidalgo smiled. "It is part of the way we honor the people who have died. It is a sweet bread, and we only make it at this time of year."

"We take some for ourselves," Mateo added, "and we leave some of the offering for the spirits to eat."

"Offering?" Benny asked.

Gloria nodded. "The offering is the most important part of Day of the Dead, and this is the first year that I got to help set it up," she said proudly. "In Spanish, we call it *ofrenda*. It's a special altar where we place things that help us remember loved ones who have died. Pictures, their favorite foods and drinks, and other things they loved when they were alive."

Henry and Jessie exchanged a glance, each

of them remembering how much their lives had changed when their parents died in a car accident. After it happened, the Alden children were supposed to go live with their grandfather, but they thought he was mean and that they wouldn't like living with him. So Henry, Jessie, Violet, and Benny ran away to the woods where they found an abandoned boxcar. They made it their home and even found their dog, Watch.

Eventually, Grandfather discovered where they were, and they realized he was not mean at all. He took the children home to live with him and his housekeeper, Mrs. McGregor. Even better, Grandfather brought the boxcar home too. He put it in his backyard for the children to use as a clubhouse.

Gloria must have noticed that her friends looked a little sad. "Don't worry," she said. "Offerings are happy things, I promise." She waved her gavel in the direction of the back porch. "Come on—I'll show you."

Mr. and Mrs. Hidalgo went back to their work, and the children tromped through the kitchen and out the sliding door to a screened-in porch. There was a table with two tiers covered in a beautiful cloth. It held framed pictures of family members, some of them from many generations ago. Four brass candlesticks sat in the form of a cross, and orange marigold petals were sprinkled around them.

"Wow," Violet said. "I love how colorful this is. You're right, Gloria—the altar doesn't feel sad at all."

"It's really a celebration of the people we love," Gloria said. "And we have the important job of honoring them. We want to welcome the spirits to visit. Besides the bread my mom is baking, we will also put out a pitcher of water to quench the spirits' thirst after their long journey. And we put out the things they loved in life. That's why we have my great-uncle's baseball cards—he loved baseball. And it's why we have this."

Gloria picked up a delicate ivory jewelry box. She opened the lid and showed it to the Aldens. "This bracelet belonged to my great-grandmother Luisa."

"It's beautiful," Jessie said. The bracelet was a chain of delicate silver flowers with charms hanging off each one. There was a tiny water jug, a marigold, and a sunbonnet. Jessie realized these charms must have marked some of their great-grandmother Luisa's favorite memories.

Gloria shook the box, and the charms on the bracelet made a jingling sound. She smiled. "That sound always makes me think of the few times I was with her. She lived so far away that we didn't get to see her much."

Mateo carefully took the jewelry box from his sister to get a closer look. "I am glad we have this," he said. "Because I was so little when she died, I don't really have a memory of her."

Henry smiled at Mateo and Gloria. "Thank you so much for sharing this with us. Family traditions are very important."

After a moment Jessie said, "You know, we had better get going if we want to celebrate Halloween before it gets too dark."

"Yes," Benny said, "and before the candy runs out!"

"Rock on," Mateo said, back in character.

Gloria laughed and adjusted her bun. "Everybody got their bags? Let's go!"

The kids filed back through the kitchen toward the front door. Just as Gloria was tying on her boots, she noticed someone was missing.

"Mateo, come on!" Gloria called. "He is always running behind," she said to the Aldens.

Mateo ran out to join them, his spiky red wig flopping down into his eyes. "I hope I get a lot of peanut butter cups," he said. "Those are my favorite."

Violet smiled. "I'm hoping for taffy," she said. The children hurried down the front path to the sidewalk. Ghosts and ninjas and lions and witches passed by, running and laughing, the beams of their flashlights bobbing across lawns. The Aldens and Hidalgos were about to join them when Violet stopped for a moment. She thought she heard something strange. It was a jingling sound. But then it was gone.

Violet decided she must have been imagining it. "Let's go!" she said.

Too Much Candy

It was dark when the children finished trick-or-treating. Their noses were red from the chilly wind, and their bags were heavy with candy. They returned to Mateo and Gloria's living room and sat in a circle on the green-striped rug.

"How about some hot apple cider to warm up?" Mr. Hidalgo asked.

"That sounds delicious, thank you," Henry said, and the others nodded in agreement. Mr. Hidalgo went to the kitchen.

"And now it's time for the best part of Halloween," Benny said. "The candy!"

Just as Benny was about to dump out his bag, Violet put her hand on his arm to stop him. While they were trick-or-treating, she had noticed that Gloria was often busy encouraging Mateo, who was a little shy, to ring the doorbell at the houses they visited. In her focus on helping him, Gloria hadn't had the chance to get much candy for herself.

"I have an idea," Violet said. "Let's pour some candy from the bags that have more into the bags that have less so that we can make sure everybody has about the same. That way it will be fair for all."

"That's a great idea, Violet," Jessie said. She was proud to have such a thoughtful sister.

Benny knew this was the right thing to do, but it was a little bit harder for him to offer his bag than it was for the others. Henry gave Benny a nod, and Benny handed his bag to Violet.

"Don't worry, Benny. There is plenty of candy for everyone," Violet said. "In fact, I should just give you all my chocolate now, since you always end up eating it anyway!"

Benny puffed out his cheeks and then laughed. "But I always ask first! Well, at least the first time."

The children giggled and worked together to divide the candy. They lifted the bags one by one until each seemed to weigh about the same. Then Violet, Benny, Gloria, and Mateo dug into their bags to find their favorite kinds of candy— peanut butter cups for Mateo, chocolate bars for Benny and Gloria, and saltwater taffy for Violet.

The Day of the Dead Mystery

They shared the caramels and chocolate-covered raisins with Henry and Jessie, and soon the only sound that filled the room was the rustling of candy wrappers.

Mr. Hidalgo came back into the living room with a tray of steaming mugs. "Now here is a happy group of children—*un grupo de niños felices*." He set the mugs on the coffee table near the couch. "Careful, please. These are hot."

"Thank you, Mr. Hidalgo," the Aldens said. When he went back into the kitchen, Mateo stood and stretched. He pulled off his rock star wig to reveal his usual short hair. The glitter around his eyes was starting to wear off.

"I think I ate too much candy," Mateo said, rubbing his stomach and pursing his lips. "I'm going to bed."

Gloria looked concerned. "Don't you want your cider?" she asked her brother.

"No, thank you," Mateo said. He picked up his bag of candy and started toward the stairs. "Good night, everyone. Thank you for coming."

"Good night, Mateo," said Henry. "Feel better soon."

"Poor Mateo," Benny said after he was gone. "Having a stomachache is no fun."

Gloria nodded. "I know. I hope he is okay."

Jessie took the mugs from the coffee table one by one and passed them out. She tried to think of something that might cheer everyone up. Across the room next to a bookshelf was a stack of what looked like art supplies. There was tissue paper and scissors, flowers, and some pastry bags like the kind Mrs. McGregor used to decorate birthday cakes for the Alden children.

"Gloria, are you planning to do a craft project?" Jessie asked.

"Well, sort of," Gloria said. She paused to take a sip of her cider and laughed when a few drops spilled on her judge's robe. "Those are some more decorations for Day of the Dead, but they aren't for our celebration here at home. In two days, we're going to a celebration at Greenfield Park, and we're taking those with us."

"Does something special happen in the park?" Benny asked. He was thinking again about the altar Gloria had shown them earlier and what

Mr. Hidalgo had said about inviting the spirits of their ancestors into their home. Benny wondered where the park fit in to the tradition.

"No, the park isn't the important part," Gloria said. "In Mexico, families usually spend the day in the cemeteries, visiting the graves of their loved ones and even spending the night there. But cemeteries in the United States have different rules about that, so people don't spend as much time in cemeteries. We find other ways to celebrate. A beautiful park is the next best thing."

"That sounds fun," Benny said. "Can we come?"

Henry cleared his throat. He hoped Gloria wouldn't think Benny was being rude. "If it's okay with your family, of course," Henry added.

A smile broke open on Gloria's face. "Of course! I think my family would love it. You know, back in Mexico we have so many aunts and uncles and lots of cousins too. But here we have only my parents and Mateo and me—and my uncle Jorge. It gets a little lonely. Of course, there are lots of other Mexican American families who will be coming to the park too. It's going to be a lot of fun!" Gloria said.

Violet's eyes kept drifting back to the colorful tissue paper. She was curious about what they planned to do with it. "Gloria, do you need help with the decorations?"

Gloria nodded. "Oh, yes, we could use it. There is a lot left to do, and if Mateo isn't feeling well, I'm not sure how much he will be able to help. Do you think you could come over tomorrow morning to work on them?"

"Oh, that's right—tomorrow's Saturday," Benny said. "No school!"

Violet looked at Jessie, and the sisters nodded. Henry said, "Yes, let's all come. If we work together, I'm sure we can help you finish the decorations in time."

"Speaking of finishing," Benny said before he took a long last drink of his cider. "That was delicious. I think I'm too full to eat any more candy."

Henry laughed. "Now, there's something I never thought I'd hear you say, Benny. I think that probably means it's time for us to say good night."

Jessie stood up and helped Gloria, Benny, and Violet put their empty mugs back on the tray.

Henry carried it to the kitchen and said good night to Mr. and Mrs. Hidalgo.

"We had fun trick-or-treating with you," Violet said as the Aldens walked out the front door. "Please tell Mateo we hope he feels better."

"I will," Gloria said. "He has to get better in time for Day of the Dead!"

One Thing Missing

When the Aldens arrived the next morning, Gloria and Mrs. Hidalgo were just finishing setting up the materials for making Day of the Dead decorations on the long table in the dining room.

"You look like yourself again," Violet said to Gloria. Now that Halloween was over, Gloria's dark, wavy hair hung down her back, and she had on her favorite gold earrings that were shaped like tiny birds.

"I'll let you kids get to work," Mrs. Hidalgo said. She opened the door that revealed stairs down to the basement. "I'll be down in my studio if you need me."

"Are you working on something new?" Henry

asked. Mrs. Hidalgo was an artist known for her colorful clay sculptures of animals. Back in September, Grandfather had taken the children to see a collection of her work at the Greenfield Art Gallery.

"Yes," she said, "an iguana!" She wiggled her fingers the way iguanas moved their long, green toes. "But don't tell Mateo. I am going to give it to him for his birthday."

Benny gave her a serious nod. "We promise to keep it a secret."

Mrs. Hidalgo waved and disappeared down the stairs. Jessie looked at Gloria. "Where *is* Mateo?" Jessie asked.

Gloria's smile faded. "Well, the good news is that he's feeling better. He was up early this morning and went out to see a friend. But I wish he were here to help make the decorations. He's usually so excited for Day of the Dead."

"Don't worry," Jessie said. "I'm sure he'll be back soon. And for now, we're here to help."

"It's going to be fun," Gloria said, cheering up. She unwrapped a package of tissue paper that included every color of the rainbow.

Violet felt her imagination start to leap and dance as she imagined all the things they could make. "Where should we begin?" she asked Gloria.

"How about by cutting some paper?" Gloria said. "In Spanish this is called *papel picado*."

She picked up a piece of orange tissue paper from the top of the pile and showed the Aldens how to fold it and use the tip of a pair of scissors to cut out shapes. When she unfolded the paper again, light shone through the holes. "We will string all these together in a line and hang them from tree to tree in the park," Gloria said. "When the breeze blows through them, they flutter in the air. I love the way they look."

"Oh, they must be so festive with all the different colors," Violet said. Benny selected a yellow piece of tissue, and Violet chose pink. They both got to work cutting out the designs.

"This reminds me of cutting paper snowflakes with Mrs. McGregor when we had a snow day last winter," Benny said. "Remember how many we made?"

The Day of the Dead Mystery

Jessie laughed. "We taped so many on the windows that Grandfather could hardly see inside when he came home."

"And poor Watch could hardly see *outside* to watch the squirrels," Benny said.

At the other end of the table, Gloria tore a piece of wax paper from a roll and spread it on a cookie sheet. Then she took the lid off a plastic food container and began carefully lifting out small white candies.

"Jessie, could you help me with the sugar skulls?" Gloria asked.

"Sure," Jessie said. She came down to Gloria's side of the table. "What are these for?"

"They are sugar skulls, or *calaveras de azúcar.* My mom did the first part by making the candies in the shape of skulls and setting them out to dry. Now we need to decorate them with frosting—the brighter and more creative, the better," she said.

"Did I hear someone say frosting?" Benny asked, perking up.

Gloria laughed. "We have a lot of decorating to do, so there's plenty of work to go around," she said. "Most of these will go on the altar. The rest we can eat, but not until tomorrow."

"Hmm," Benny said. He was much more interested in the eating than the decorating. "I think I'd better stick to paper."

Jessie laughed. "That's okay, Benny." She turned back to Gloria. "How do the skulls fit in to the celebration?" she asked. Skulls had always seemed spooky to her, but she could tell they meant something different to Gloria and her family.

"In our culture," Gloria said, "death isn't something to be afraid of. It's just a natural part of life. Bright colors and silly frosting faces painted on the skulls, plus music and games and good food, all help us remember to celebrate the people we lost instead of being sad."

Gloria helped Jessie spoon red, yellow, and purple frosting into separate pastry bags. Then Jessie began to pipe designs on the sugar skulls and place them one by one on the cookie sheet to dry.

"Last but not least, we have the flowers," Gloria said. Henry said he would help with those. Gloria opened a new package of orange tissue paper and

showed Henry how to fold a stack of sheets in an accordion pattern, tie them at the center, and fluff out the layers of paper until it looked like a marigold blossom.

"My mom will add these to the altar along with real marigold petals. The tradition says that the bright orange color and the beautiful scent of the flowers help guide spirits back to earth on this special night when they can visit us."

Violet looked up from the paper she was cutting. "Gloria, those flowers remind me of the flowers on your great-grandmother's bracelet."

"You're right," Gloria said. "Maybe looking at it will give us some more ideas for the patterns on the tissue paper. I'm going to get it." Gloria left the dining room and walked through the kitchen to the altar on the back porch.

A moment later she came running back in. "The bracelet!" she cried. "It's gone!"

Henry set down the paper flower he was working on. "Are you sure?" he asked. "Maybe it fell on the floor. We'll help you look." The Alden children went with Gloria back to the porch.

Benny got down on his knees and crawled under the tablecloth that hung from the table. Then he stuck his head back out. "I'm sorry, Gloria," he said. "There's nothing under here."

Gloria stared at the empty jewelry box on the altar in disbelief. Then she put her head in her hands.

"Oh, I knew I should have listened to Mamá. She said we should put the bracelet back in the jewelry box in her closet until the big day, but I wanted to be able to look at it." Her voice sounded thick, like she was trying not to cry. "We have to find it. I can't tell my dad about this."

Violet put her hand on Gloria's arm. "Don't worry—we'll help you. And if we don't find it, I'm sure your father will understand."

Gloria shook her head. "I don't think so. If I tell him it's gone, then he will have to tell my uncle Jorge. They have always argued about which one of them should get to have the bracelet, especially since Uncle Jorge had to move in with us when he lost his job at the library. They are worried about money. And of course everyone loved my great-grandmother Luisa, but we have so few things that belonged to her here in America. Everything is back in Mexico. Knowing it's gone will just make things worse between Papá and Uncle Jorge."

"All right," Jessie said. "Let's stay calm. The bracelet can't have gone far. Let's make a plan. First, we should figure out if anything else is missing from the altar."

Gloria looked carefully over the two tiers of the table. The brass candlesticks were still there, as well as the picture frames and the other items for each family member being remembered. "Everything else is here," she said.

While the rest of the children looked at the items on the altar, Henry was looking in another direction, out the window of the porch. "Look at that," he said, pointing outside. "The gate is open."

Gloria furrowed her brow. "That's strange," she said. "That gate connects our yard with the Hayes's house next door."

Benny looked out the side window at the blue house with white trim. "You mean that house there?" he asked, pointing. Then Benny gasped. "Someone's looking at us!"

The other four children turned in Benny's direction and looked out the side window just in time to see a woman's face peering down at them from the second-floor window. When she saw them looking at her, she jerked the curtain closed.

Jessie wheeled around to Gloria, her eyes wide.

"Do you know that woman?"

Gloria shook her head. "Not really. Her name is Mrs. Hayes, but we've never really talked to her. She keeps to herself. Her daughter, Tina, is the same age as Mateo, and they play together. Never at Tina's house though."

Jessie looked at Violet and then at Henry. "I think Mrs. Hayes might be our first suspect," Jessie said.

A Surprising Assessment

"Are you saying you think Mrs. Hayes *stole* the bracelet?" Benny asked. "But why would she want to do that?"

Henry held up his hands. "Well, let's slow down. We don't know what happened, and it wouldn't be fair to accuse someone of something without any proof. Plus, it doesn't look like someone broke in— nothing else is missing. But *if* someone stole the bracelet, maybe Mrs. Hayes, maybe someone else, it might be because that person needed money."

"But how would she—or he—know the bracelet was worth something?" Violet asked.

Jessie thought about this for a moment. "The thief wouldn't know for sure, but a jeweler would. Remember when Grandfather helped Mrs. McGregor get her uncle's pocket watch repaired? They took it to the jeweler, and he told them what kind of gold it was made of and how much he would pay her if she wanted to sell it."

Henry added, "That's right. Mrs. McGregor was so surprised by the amount of money that she made Grandfather drive her straight to the bank so she could put it in the safe deposit box."

"If the thief took the bracelet to the jeweler," Violet said, "maybe the jeweler would remember seeing it."

"We should go ask him!" Gloria said. She turned back to the altar and carefully took down the framed photo of her great-grandmother. In the photo, Luisa wore a red dress with sleeves that stopped just below her elbows. On her left wrist was the bracelet. "We can show him this picture," Gloria said. She pulled her empty backpack down from a hook by the back door and carefully zipped the framed picture inside.

"Let's go!" Benny said, and the kids raced through the kitchen and dining room to the front door.

A Surprising Assessment

While the Aldens put on their shoes, Gloria called down to her mother to tell her they were taking a break from the decorations and going for a bike ride.

"I'll get my bike and meet you out front," Gloria said as they went down the front steps.

The Alden children ran home and got their bikes. After they met back up with Gloria, the group pedaled as fast as they could toward Greenfield Jewelers on Main Street. Though it was the first day of November, the sun shone on their faces and kept them warm. It was exciting to have an important mission, and the Aldens had a feeling they were getting on the right track to solve the mystery.

"There it is!" Henry said when the gold letters on the Greenfield Jewelers sign came into view. He was riding in front and pulled his bike to the curb. The others followed and locked their bikes to the rack on the sidewalk, catching their breath before they went inside the small shop.

"We'll let you do the talking, Gloria," Jessie said. "But we're here to help if you need us."

Gloria nodded. She opened the door, and a little

bell jangled as the children filed inside.

"Good morning," said a tall man with gold wire glasses. He was standing behind the glass case at the back of the shop, which was filled with sparkling gemstone rings, watches, and necklaces and bracelets of many colors. Soft violin music played over the speakers.

"Good morning," Gloria said, using her most grown-up voice. She glanced nervously at Violet.

Violet gave her a thumbs-up and whispered, "You can do it."

Gloria nodded. She unzipped her backpack and took out the framed picture. Then she set it carefully on top of the glass case.

"How can I help you, young lady?" the man said.

Gloria pointed to her great-grandmother's wrist. "The bracelet in this picture belongs to my family, but it has gone missing," Gloria said. "I don't know if it was stolen. But if it was, I thought, maybe, that the person would have brought it here to find out how much it is worth."

The jeweler took a closer look at the photo. Then he nodded. "I do recognize this—in fact, I just saw

it yesterday. I am so sorry to hear that it has gone missing." He looked up at Gloria. "Did you know that it is worth quite a bit of money?"

Gloria's eyes widened. "No, I didn't know that. We've never cared about the money part. My great-grandmother actually made this bracelet herself. She was known as a very skilled artisan all across the region, and people would come from miles away to buy her creations as gifts for their loved ones. We are very proud of her work, and that makes this bracelet priceless to us, no matter how much it is worth."

The jeweler nodded kindly. "I understand what you mean. I became a jeweler because my father and grandfather were jewelers too, back in Poland. Family traditions are very important. If you'll excuse me for a moment, I'll go into the back and check the records to see who brought the bracelet in."

Gloria nodded, and the jeweler went through a curtain into the back room. The Aldens came to stand beside their friend, who was looking very anxious.

Benny took a small chocolate bar left over from

A Surprising Assessment

Halloween from his pocket and put it in Gloria's hand. "You look like you could use this," Benny said. "Don't worry. I just know we're going to get to the bottom of this."

"Thanks, Benny," Gloria said.

The jeweler came back to the counter holding a record book. He ran his finger down the page until he came to an entry for the previous day. "This says a man named Martín Hidalgo brought the bracelet in yesterday."

Gloria's face went pale. "Martín Hidalgo?" she said. "But...that's my father."

"Oh, dear," the jeweler said. "How strange."

Gloria thought for a moment, trying to decide what question to ask next. "When he brought it in, did he tell you he wanted to sell it?"

"No," the jeweler said. "He did ask me to appraise the piece, which is how I knew when you showed me the picture that it is considered very valuable. Mr. Hidalgo listened to what I told him, then said thank you and put the bracelet back in his pocket. I wish I could give you more information, but that's all I have to tell you about what happened."

"Thank you," Gloria said. "That's very helpful."

"Good luck," the jeweler said. "I hope you find it."

"Me too," Gloria said.

"You kids have a nice afternoon," the jeweler said as the kids waved good-bye. Back on the sidewalk, Henry knelt down and unlocked the bikes one by one from the metal rack.

"I don't understand it," Gloria said, pulling nervously on the end of her long braid. "My dad took the bracelet? Why would he even think about selling it?"

Violet thought back to the previous night when the children had returned from trick-or-treating. Mr. Hidalgo had been so kind, making the hot cider for them and joking about their candy. He just didn't seem like the kind of person who would take the bracelet without asking his family first. "There has to be an explanation," Violet said. "Is it possible your dad still has it, or that he gave it to your mom to wear?"

Gloria shrugged. "I guess so, but it isn't really her style."

"Either way," Jessie said, "I think you should ask

A Surprising Assessment

them about it. Tell them that you noticed it was gone from the altar and that you've been worried about it."

Gloria looked uncertain, but finally she nodded. "You're probably right," she said as she threw her leg over her bike. "Let's head back to my house."

The children began pedaling back up Main Street toward their neighborhood. The sidewalk was getting crowded with shoppers and people going to the movies or out to lunch at the Greenfield Diner. Thinking of lunch made Benny's stomach growl so loud that Violet, who was pedaling next to him, heard it and giggled. On the next block they passed Superdog. It was Benny's favorite hot dog stand because you could choose from four kinds of mustard and three kinds of relish. Now his mouth was really watering.

"Is anybody else hungry?" Benny asked.

Gloria looked at him over her shoulder, and her face brightened. "You read my mind, Benny," she said. "But I've got something better than hot dogs for you. My mom is making tamales!"

"What are tamales?" Benny said.

The Day of the Dead Mystery

"You had tamales once at a party," Jessie told her brother. "But you might have been too young to remember. They have cheese or meat or vegetables wrapped in dough, and they are cooked inside a corn husk."

"The dough is made from corn flour, or masa," Gloria added. "You are in for a treat. My mom's tamales are the best!"

Just thinking about trying the new food made Benny pedal faster, and soon the children were pulling into Gloria's driveway. They piled their bikes next to the garage and climbed the stairs to the back porch, where Gloria had set up the altar.

The tamales had gotten Gloria excited, but seeing the empty place on the altar made her shoulders fall. The Aldens could see that she was worried about how to ask her parents about the bracelet. She unzipped her backpack and pulled out her great-grandmother Luisa's picture, gently placing it back in its spot. She also picked up the empty jewelry box to put it back where it belonged, but when she did the lid came open, and she heard a jingling sound.

A Surprising Assessment

"I can't believe it!" Gloria said. "The bracelet is back!"

The children crowded closer to Gloria to see. Henry was the first one to notice that Gloria wasn't quite right. "That is *a* bracelet," he started to say.

Gloria finished the thought. "But this bracelet is *not* my great-grandmother's!"

CHAPTER 5

Little to Go On

Just then, Henry noticed that Mateo was standing in the doorway between the kitchen and the back porch. "Oh, hi, Mateo," Henry said. "I didn't see you there."

Mateo nodded but didn't say anything.

"When did you get home?" Gloria asked him. She wasn't sure whether to tell him about the missing bracelet or ask him about this mysterious new one that had shown up in the box. Mateo had been acting very strangely lately, disappearing with his friend and not helping out with Day of the Dead preparations. As Gloria was deciding what to say next, Mrs. Hidalgo called the children inside.

Gloria closed the jewelry box and left it on the

altar. The children crowded into the kitchen as Mrs. Hidalgo removed the lid from a large pot, releasing a big cloud of steam.

"Hello!" she said. "In a few minutes it's going to be time for Mateo and Gloria to say good-bye for now. We have friends coming over for dinner this evening. But first I need some volunteers to taste test the tamales."

Benny's hand shot up, and Mrs. Hidalgo smiled at him. "Benny, I thought you might be interested in these." She used a pair of tongs to pull the tamales from the steamer basket and placed them on two plates.

"These smell delicious," Jessie said.

"This kind has pork and red pepper," Gloria said, pointing at the first plate. "And this one is just cheese."

Gloria served a tamal to each of her friends. Then she looked around. "Now where did Mateo go this time?" She sounded frustrated.

"Over here," Mateo said. He was still standing in the doorway looking at the altar. Gloria and Jessie shared a glance. Both of them thought it was odd that he still hadn't joined them at the table.

"Do you want a tamal, Mateo?" Gloria asked.

"No, thank you," Mateo said. Without another word, he walked back out to the porch. They heard the back door open and close.

Benny whispered so that Mrs. Hidalgo would not be able to hear him. "Does anyone else think Mateo is acting strange?"

"Yes!" the children whispered back in unison.

Mrs. Hidalgo came over to the table. "Well?" she said. "What do you think?"

"Five stars!" Benny said, his mouth full of pork and masa.

"So tasty!" Violet said.

Mrs. Hidalgo grinned. "Well, someday when we have more time, you should join us for a full meal. We love to eat around here, don't we, Gloria?"

Gloria smiled back at her mother. But she was still thinking about the bracelet they had found. Why would someone—her dad?—take the real bracelet and put another one in its place? And where had he gotten the new one?

"And now it's time to say good-bye," Mrs.

Hidalgo said. "I need Gloria's help to get the table ready. Uncle Jorge and your father will be home in an hour!"

The Aldens carried their dishes to the sink and thanked Mrs. Hidalgo again for the food. Gloria walked them to the back door. As they passed the altar, she took down the jewelry box and handed it to them.

"Take this with you," Gloria said. "Maybe you can keep investigating where the new bracelet came from."

Jessie nodded and took the box. She put it in the pocket of her jacket, and Gloria went back inside and closed the door. The Aldens walked their bikes down to the sidewalk, but as they were about to ride off for home, they saw Mateo and a girl with curly red hair and white high-tops walking slowly toward them on the sidewalk. The two children were looking down at the ground and in the grass as they moved. They would have run straight into the front wheel of Henry's bike if he hadn't said, "Hey, careful!"

"Oh, hi," Mateo said. He turned to his friend.

"Tina, these are the new friends I was telling you about, the Aldens. They live down the block. Henry, Jessie, Violet, and Benny, this is Tina."

Tina smiled and waved. "It's nice to meet you," she said.

"You too," Jessie said in her usual friendly voice. But she was a little distracted by what she remembered Gloria telling them about Tina. She was the daughter of the woman who had been watching them through the upstairs window of the house next door. And Tina and Mateo never played at Tina's house. Something about that just seemed funny. Jessie wondered if it might be a clue to what had happened to the bracelet.

"Are you looking for something?" Violet asked.

"We—um—thought we might be able to find some candy on the sidewalk that trick-or-treaters dropped," Mateo said.

"But didn't you eat enough candy last night?" Benny asked. "You had such a bad stomachache." Benny knew all about those kinds of stomachaches, and he wanted to help Mateo avoid getting one all over again.

Mateo looked surprised for a second, as if he had forgotten about feeling sick the night before. "Well, that won't be a problem," he said to Benny, "because we haven't found any candy."

"All right," Henry said, looking a little confused. "Well, good luck. It's almost time for dinner, so we are heading home. I think Gloria and your mother are looking for you."

Mateo nodded. "Okay, I'd better go inside. I'll see you later."

The Aldens pedaled home and put their bikes in the garage. Watch heard them coming and ran to the back door and barked, so Henry let him out. The sun was going down, and the sky was striped with peach and pink light. Mrs. McGregor called out the kitchen window that they had ten minutes before it was time to wash up and come inside for the evening. The Aldens knew they didn't have a moment to waste. They rushed across the backyard to their boxcar. It was their favorite place to hold meetings when they were investigating a mystery.

Inside, the children sat in a circle on the floor. Benny sat next to Watch and rubbed the dog's head, which made Watch's tail thump quietly on the floor. Jessie brought a camping lantern over and set it in the center of the circle. Then she took the jewelry box from her coat pocket and removed the bracelet.

"I want to take a closer look at this bracelet," Jessie said.

It was hard to see in the dim light, but even still it was clear this bracelet was not the same as Gloria's great-grandmother's. It was a charm bracelet, like the first one, but this one had charms that looked like coins—gold, silver, and bronze. It was hard to make out the designs on the charms. The new bracelet also had a different style of clasp—a long, flat rectangle.

Benny lifted the bracelet in his palm and turned it over. "Hey," he said, "this has writing on it!"

He passed the bracelet to Henry. "You're right, Benny. There's something engraved on the back of the clasp, but the words are too tiny to see."

"I have an idea!" Violet said. She got up from the circle and went to the shelves where the Aldens stored some of the toys and games they kept in the boxcar. Inside one of the baskets was an old-fashioned magnifying glass. "This should help," she said.

Henry took the magnifying glass and held it above the bracelet. "Good thinking, Violet," he said. He leaned as close as he could to the weak light coming from the lantern. "It says, 'Thank you for all you do.' And then there's a name. 'G.S. Banks.'"

Henry sat back and looked at the others. "What do you think it means?"

Jessie shook her head. "I have no idea," she said. "But whoever put this bracelet on the altar is probably the owner. So if we can figure out who G.S. Banks is, maybe that will lead us to him. Or her."

"That's right," Henry said. "The owner of the bracelet is probably a woman, but the person who gave it to her could be a woman *or* a man."

Violet shook her head. "I still have so many questions. We know that Gloria's father took the first bracelet to the jeweler. But he didn't leave it there—he took it with him. So what did he do with it? Put it back on the altar?"

"If he did," Henry said, "that could mean

someone else took it and put this bracelet in its place. What I don't know is why someone would do that."

Just then they heard Mrs. McGregor calling from the back door. "Children, time to come inside!"

Henry grabbed the magnifying glass and the bracelet, and the children traipsed through the back door of the Alden house. They washed up at the sink, and Benny and Henry went into the dining room to set the table. Jessie poured fresh water and food into Watch's bowls, but Watch wasn't so interested in dog food. Like always, he positioned himself where he was most likely to catch delicious people food—next to Benny's chair.

As Mrs. McGregor served the children helpings of her famous vegetarian lasagna and garlic bread, Grandfather asked about their day.

"I bumped into Mrs. Hidalgo at the grocery store," Grandfather said. "She told me that you helped Gloria and Mateo get ready for Day of the Dead. It sounds like they have quite the celebration planned."

Violet nodded. "And Gloria invited us to join

them for it tomorrow. Is it okay if we go?"

"I think that would be very nice," Grandfather said.

Jessie and Henry shared a glance. They were worried that it wouldn't feel much like a celebration if the bracelet were still missing.

The children were hungry from their busy day, and each of them ate two helpings of lasagna. Then they cleared the table without being asked and even put on the kettle to make a cup of tea for Mrs. McGregor.

"Well!" she said. "I like these new friendships you've made with Gloria and Mateo. I think they are having a good influence on you!"

She smiled and rose to help Henry rinse the plates and load the dishwasher. Violet and Benny wiped the table, and Jessie pulled the heavy trash bag out of the can. When Grandfather took it outside to the bin, Jessie got an idea: the name on the bracelet could be the name of someone who lived in Greenfield! She went into Grandfather Alden's study and took the phone book down from his bookshelf.

Settled together on the floor of the living room, Henry, Violet, and Benny listened to Jessie's plan for tracking down the bracelet's owner. She showed them the phone book.

"If we can find the person in this book, maybe we can talk to them," Jessie said. "What's the name again?"

"G.S. Banks," Henry said, peering through the magnifying glass.

Jessie flipped through the book until she came to the *B* section. "Bader, Baelstrom...here it is—Banks." She trailed her finger down the column of names. There were a lot of people with the last name Banks in the Greenfield region. "There is a Frances, a Frederick, and a Herbert. But no G.S. Banks."

"How strange," Violet said. "I guess the bracelet could have been a gift from someone in another city."

"In which case we'll never find the person this way," Henry said. "We only have a phone book for Greenfield."

"Hang on," Benny said. He carefully took the bracelet from Henry and looked at it through the magnifying glass. "There's more writing here on one of the charms. This charm says 'fifteen years' on it. Could it be for a wedding anniversary?"

The other children shrugged. They couldn't say for sure, but a wedding anniversary didn't seem quite right. The inscription didn't say anything about love or marriage. Next Benny showed them some of the symbols on the backs of the other charms.

Grandfather came in to read his paper by the fireplace, his favorite evening activity. "What are you up to, kids?"

Henry decided it was time to tell their grandfather the whole story. Maybe he could help them figure out where the bracelet had come from. So the children filled Grandfather in on everything to do with Day of the Dead, the Hidalgo family's altar, and of course the missing bracelet and the new one that had shown up in its place.

Grandfather listened carefully. A slight smile came over his face. "Well, if anyone can solve this mystery, it's my grandchildren," he said. He glanced at the clock on the mantel. "Though it's getting pretty late. Maybe you should get a good night's sleep and start fresh in the morning."

Henry nodded. "I think Grandfather might be right," he said.

Grandfather stood up and folded the paper under his arm. The children were surprised because he hadn't even begun to read it, but he seemed distracted by something. "Now, I'm sorry to leave you," Grandfather said, "but there's something I've got to take care of."

CHAPTER 6

Breakfast Breakthrough

The Aldens took their grandfather's advice and went to bed early, but the next morning they weren't feeling any closer to understanding what had happened with the bracelet.

Benny rubbed his eyes as he stood at the foot of Jessie's bed and waited for her to put on her slippers. "I thought for sure it would come to me in a dream," he said.

Jessie laughed. "I'm afraid solving mysteries doesn't quite work that way, Benny. We just don't have enough information to make any progress yet."

"Well, we aren't going to find any more up here," Henry said, coming into the girls' room. He was already dressed.

Breakfast Breakthrough

Violet got out of bed and combed her hair into pigtails. "Let's get moving," she said.

Benny, Violet, and Jessie went down to breakfast, but they were surprised to find that the house was quiet. Watch was snoozing on the living room floor. Mrs. McGregor was gone to her League of Women Voters meeting, and Grandfather was not in his study. As they stood in the kitchen, wondering where to begin, Violet noticed a blue piece of paper on the table. There was some money attached with a paper clip.

Kids,

I'm sorry to miss you this morning. You have been working so hard on your case. Why don't you take this money and treat yourselves to breakfast in town. Have fun today, but be sure to be home by 5:30 p.m. I have a surprise for you.

Love,
Grandfather

"Well, this should be fun!" Violet said, showing the note to her brothers and sister. "Where should we go?"

"How about the Crispy Biscuit?" Benny asked, his eyes growing big. He recited their slogan from the radio. "'The best breakfast in Greenfield!'"

"Sounds good to me," Henry agreed. "I'm so hungry I think I'll order the Lumberjack Breakfast."

"I want waffles," Violet said, "with berries and whipped cream. What about you, Jessie?"

"Hmm," Jessie said, "I think I will have to look at the menu." Jessie always liked to have all the information before she made a decision.

The three older Aldens looked at Benny. "No one has to ask me what I'm going to order," Benny said with a smile. "You know it will be chocolate chip pancakes every time!"

The children laughed, and Jessie and Violet, still in their pajamas, ran upstairs to get dressed. Then the Aldens put on their jackets and grabbed their bikes from the garage. It was a cloudy day but a little warmer than it had been the day before, with no rain in the forecast. Perfect bike-riding weather. As the children pedaled toward Main Street, they passed Greenfield Cemetery. It was at the top of a hill, full of tall trees and surrounded by a wrought iron fence.

Jessie was the first to notice that the usually gray and quiet cemetery was full of activity. "Look!" she called to her brothers and sister. "I guess Day of the Dead has already started."

The Aldens slowed their bikes and turned in the direction she was pointing. Several families were gathered throughout the rows of headstones. Some were setting up folding chairs. Others were hanging brightly colored decorations from the branches of the trees. Though they were in a place that Jessie had always thought of as sad—a cemetery full of people who had died—the families did not look upset. Instead, they laughed and hugged one another, clearly happy to be together to celebrate the special day.

Henry, Jessie, and Violet picked up speed again, but Benny fell behind. He wasn't looking at the cemetery but at a sign for a business across the street. Next to the words was a symbol he recognized from somewhere, but he couldn't quite remember where.

Breakfast Breakthrough

"Come on, Benny!" Jessie called. "Your pancakes are waiting!"

Benny smiled and pedaled harder to catch up with his siblings.

As usual, a show tune was playing on the sound system when the Aldens walked in to the Crispy Biscuit and found a table by the window. The owner, Chef Ralph, was a big fan of musicals, and he sometimes played "Name That Tune" with customers, promising a discount on their breakfast if they could identify the song he played. Mrs. McGregor was very good at this game—she guessed right every time—but the children didn't always know the older songs. Still, they loved the jolly atmosphere of the restaurant.

The dining room was filled with the delicious scent of bacon and pancakes. When Chef Ralph saw the Aldens come in, he scurried out to their table to say hello.

"Hi, kids! Did you put your listening ears on before you came? I just hit play on one I *know* you will get."

Ralph waited, his spatula in the air, while the

children closed their eyes and strained to hear the lyrics. A man was singing about an impossible dream and an unreachable star. After a minute, Chef Ralph said, "Well?"

The Aldens looked at each other and shrugged. "I'm sorry," Henry said, "but we don't know this one."

"Ah, well," Ralph said, "if this one ever comes to the Greenfield Playhouse, you have to go. *Man of La Mancha* is inspired by the story of Don Quixote, a man who never gave up hope."

"I think I would like that story," Violet said with a smile. "It has a good message for us today." The other children nodded—they knew they could not give up hope of finding the bracelet.

"Now to breakfast," Ralph said. "What can I get you?"

Henry, Violet, and Benny ordered the dishes they'd chosen, and Jessie finally settled on pigs in a blanket. Chef Ralph headed back to the kitchen, and they leaned in so they could hear each other over the sounds of silverware and the crooning singer.

Jessie took her notebook out of her bag and

opened it on the table. "Let's make a list of what we actually know," she said.

"Good idea," Henry said. "The first thing is, whoever took the bracelet knew where it was. Nothing else in the house was disturbed, so it's not as if just any thief broke in."

Jessie nodded and wrote down, "Thief knew about bracelet."

"That's right," Violet said. "So who knew? Gloria's dad, Mr. Hidalgo. And we know he took it to be appraised at the jeweler."

"Gloria's Uncle Jorge knew the bracelet was there too," added Jessie. She wrote down their names.

Benny nodded. "And what about the neighbor who was watching us from her window? Tina's mother, Mrs. Hayes? She could see the altar from there, and if there was enough light, she might have been able to see the bracelet when Gloria put it there."

Henry nodded, thinking about this. "It would have been pretty hard to see from that distance, but it's possible."

"And the back gate was open," Benny added.

Jessie added Mrs. Hayes to the list as well.

"True," Violet said, "but the only thing that happened with Mrs. Hayes was that she gave us a strange look. I don't think that's much to go on at all."

The food arrived, and the children dug in, still thinking. Jessie dipped a bite of sausage wrapped in pancake into the syrup and popped it in her mouth. Then her eyes widened. She finished chewing and said, "Maybe we're asking the wrong question. It doesn't matter so much who knew about the bracelet as who put this new bracelet in place of Gloria's great-grandmother's."

Jessie took the jewelry box out of her coat pocket and opened it in the center of the table. The Aldens leaned in to look it over once more, this time in much better light.

Benny wiped the melted chocolate from his fingertips and picked up the bracelet to examine it more closely. He looked up in surprise at his siblings. "I *thought* I recognized this!" he said. Benny pointed to a symbol on one of the charms. "When we were riding our bikes by the cemetery on the way here, I saw a sign across the street that had this same symbol on it."

Jessie thought back to their bike ride. Benny had slowed down near the local bank. "That's right!" she exclaimed. "That's the symbol for Greenfield Savings Banks!"

"G.S. Banks," said Henry, putting the pieces together. "Nice work, Benny."

The children asked a waitress for the check, and Violet ate her last strawberry and finished her juice. "That means the bracelet was not a gift from a person," Violet said. "It was a gift from the bank. Maybe the owner of the bracelet works there!"

Jessie snapped her fingers. "Of course! The 'fifteen years' is the number of years the person who got this worked at the bank."

CHAPTER 7

Another Theft?

Outside the Crispy Biscuit, the children unlocked their bikes and rode to the main branch of Greenfield Savings Banks, a brick building on the other end of Main Street. A man on his way out held the fancy wooden door open for them as they walked in. At the teller window, Jessie took out the jewelry box.

"Good morning," said the teller. She was a tall woman wearing round red glasses and a name tag that said *Andrea*. "How may I help you?"

Jessie pushed the bracelet across the counter. "We were wondering if you could help us figure out where this bracelet came from. See right here?" Jessie pointed at the charm Benny had noticed. "It has the bank's logo on it."

Another Theft?

Andrea took a closer look. "I haven't seen this particular one, but you're right about the logo. This does look like a work anniversary gift. The bank gives one out to female employees who have been here for fifteen years. The only women who have worked at this branch that long are Shelly Simms down there"—the teller pointed to the woman a few windows down—"Maureen Traister, who works in the back office, and Helena Hayes. She's off today."

Jessie looked at her siblings. All of their eyes were wide as moons. Helena Hayes was Mrs. Hayes—Tina's mother and the neighbor who had been watching them from her window.

"Thank you," Jessie called to the teller as the children raced outside and hopped on their bikes, heading for their neighborhood. They couldn't wait to tell Gloria and Mateo what they had learned.

At the Hidalgos' house, Violet rang the doorbell. When the door opened, she jumped back in surprise. "Wow!" Violet said.

"Yikes!" said Benny.

Gloria and Mateo laughed and opened the door for the Aldens to come inside. Their faces were painted white with black outlines and designs around their eyes and mouths that made them look like skulls.

"How do you like our Catrina makeup?" Mateo asked.

"It's another tradition for Day of the Dead," Gloria said. "People paint their faces this way to help us honor and connect with the dead. I'm sorry if I startled you. It's not supposed to be scary."

"I'm not scared," Benny said, sheepishly. "Just surprised."

"I don't think it's scary at all," Jessie said. She noticed the delicate swooping lines and shapes painted across Gloria's forehead and said, "I think it's beautiful."

"It helps when your mom is an artist," Gloria said. "Our Catrina makeup is always the best—right, Mateo?"

"Right!" he said. Mateo had an elaborate spider web across one side of his face, and dark blue rings painted around his eyes. "I'm going to show it to Tina," he said before he ran out through the kitchen. Gloria watched him go and rolled her eyes. "So much for Mateo," she said. "But I'm happy to see you. Does this mean you have some new information for us about the bracelet?"

The Aldens explained what they'd learned about the connection between the replacement bracelet and Greenfield Savings Banks. And the information about Mrs. Hayes.

Gloria's black-painted mouth dropped open in shock. "I can't believe Mrs. Hayes would steal my great-grandmother's bracelet! Do you still have it with you?"

Jessie nodded and showed Gloria the jewelry box.

"Well, I say we go over there right now and ask her," Gloria said. "This has gone on long enough."

Henry thought for a moment. "I think we should do that too, but let's be careful. It's pretty serious to accuse someone of stealing unless you're absolutely sure they did it. There still might be another explanation."

"I hope you're right," Gloria said.

The children tromped back out across the lawn to the front door of the Hayes house.

The Day of the Dead Mystery

Gloria rang the doorbell. After a moment, the door opened, and the woman inside cried out, "Oh, goodness!"

Once again, Gloria had forgotten that her Catrina makeup might come as a surprise. "I am sorry if I startled you, Mrs. Hayes. I'm dressed up for the celebration today. Day of the Dead."

Mrs. Hayes gave Gloria a weak smile and nodded. "Yes, I've heard about that," she said. She still looked a little worried about the makeup though.

Gloria took the bracelet out of the jewelry box. She showed it to Mrs. Hayes. "We've been wondering—is this your bracelet?"

Mrs. Hayes stepped out into the daylight on the porch. "Why, yes. That does look just like my bracelet. I got it as a gift for my service to the bank. But I hardly ever wear it." She looked up at Gloria, confused. "How did it get from my house to yours?"

"That's what we came to ask you," Gloria said. "This jewelry box used to contain a very special bracelet that belonged to my great-grandmother. We only take it out this time of year, at Day of the Dead, in order to put it on our altar in her honor.

Yesterday, that bracelet went missing. A while later, *this* bracelet showed up in its place."

"I don't understand," Mrs. Hayes said.

"We saw you watching us from the window yesterday," Violet said, trying to sound as friendly as she could. "We thought maybe...you saw the bracelet and decided to take it?"

Mrs. Hayes's eyes went wide. "Steal it? I would never do that." She took a deep breath. "I'm sorry your family's heirloom went missing," she said to Gloria. "And I'm sorry if you felt I was staring at you. It's just that I don't know very much about Day of the Dead, and I was curious about all the things your family has been doing to celebrate."

"Oh," Gloria said, surprised. She looked quickly at the others and could tell they were thinking the same thing: Mrs. Hayes really did seem confused. She was not the one who had taken the bracelet. "Well, if you are free this afternoon, you should join us at Greenfield Park for our big celebration. There will be lots of music and food. And that way you can learn more about our traditions."

Mrs. Hayes smiled and nodded. "I'd like that,"

she said. "One thing I've always loved about this neighborhood is all the different kinds of people who live here. We're so lucky to be in a place where we can learn things from each other."

"Life would be pretty boring if everyone was the same, wouldn't it?" Gloria said.

"Yes, it would," Mrs. Hayes said. "Well, good luck with your search, and I'll look forward to seeing you at the party."

Gloria nodded. She was about to give the bracelet back then paused. "Mrs. Hayes," she said. "Do you mind if we hold on to your bracelet just a little longer? I think it might help us solve our mystery."

"Yes, of course," Mrs. Hayes said. "I didn't even know it was missing until you brought it back to me. If you think it will help you solve your mystery, go ahead and hang on to it."

The children thanked Mrs. Hayes and then walked back across the lawn to the Hidalgos' house. Along the way, they talked things over.

"Why would someone steal a bracelet from your porch, and then steal a bracelet from the house next door and put it where the first one was?"

Henry asked. "It seems like we know even less now than we did before!"

"Yeah," Benny said, "now we have two stolen things and zero culprits!"

"But we do know something," Jessie said, "which is that Mrs. Hayes wasn't the one to take the first bracelet."

"She was very surprised when we showed her the bracelet from the bank," said Violet. "She doesn't seem to have anything to hide."

Jessie nodded. "I think we can cross her off our suspect list."

Gloria, who had been walking quietly, finally spoke up. "I think I know exactly who we should talk to next."

A Sweet Surprise

The Alden children followed Gloria up her driveway, past the pile of bikes, and into the backyard, where Mateo and Tina were playing on a tire swing hanging from the maple tree. Tina sat on the swing, and Mateo turned her around and around until the rope was tangled up on itself. Then he let go, and Tina spun faster and faster. Both of them laughed with glee.

But when Mateo saw the look on his sister's face, his laugh died away. "Hi, Gloria," he said nervously.

Gloria held out the bracelet so both Mateo and Tina could see it. "It's time for you to tell me the truth, Mateo," Gloria said. "The *whole* truth."

The Day of the Dead Mystery

Mateo looked at Tina, and she nodded. He took a deep breath. "The truth is that I took the bracelet."

Gloria gasped. The Alden children looked at each other in surprise, but they didn't say anything. They knew it was important for Gloria and Mateo to talk things out without being interrupted.

"Why would you do that?" Gloria asked. Her voice quavered as if she might start to cry.

"I wasn't trying to steal it or anything like that," Mateo explained. "The night we went trick-or-treating all together, when you were telling the stories about Great-Grandma Luisa, I started to feel sad. You have lots of memories of her, but I don't. I was too young the last time we visited Mexico. So I decided to wear the bracelet while we were out—just for a couple hours—because it helped me feel a little closer to her. I planned to put it back when we got home, I swear!"

"Oh, Mateo," Gloria said. She felt bad about how angry she had been with her brother. It was easy to forget that he could feel left out of the memories sometimes.

"Except," Mateo continued, "when we got home

from trick-or-treating, I realized the bracelet must have fallen off somewhere in the neighborhood."

"That's why you two were walking in that strange way on the sidewalk yesterday," Jessie said. "You were looking for it."

Finally, Tina spoke up. "Yes. But we didn't find it. I think we've been over every inch of this neighborhood. I just don't understand where it could be. I've been telling Mateo he should just tell you the truth."

"I should have listened," Mateo said. "I'm very sorry."

Gloria hugged her brother. "The most important thing is that you're telling the truth now," she said.

"That's right," Jessie said. Henry nodded.

"And where does your mother's bracelet come in?" Violet asked Tina.

"Mateo asked if I could help him find something to put in the box, just until we could find the real bracelet. I didn't think my mom would miss it because she never wears it, and I didn't think anyone would look inside the box because Day of the Dead was still a day away."

"Well, at least that mystery is solved," Violet said.

"But there's one mystery left: Where is the first bracelet?" Henry asked.

The children thought back to the night of Halloween. Violet remembered that she had heard something jingling as they'd walked out the door of Gloria and Mateo's house. She told the others about it. "That sound must have been the bracelet. I heard it all through the night, when we were walking around, and even when we came back home."

"Which means," Gloria said to Mateo, "that you must have still had the bracelet on when we got home."

"Mateo," Henry said, an idea flashing through his mind, "have you checked your candy bag?"

Mateo nodded. "I checked it when I went to my room after trick-or-treating. No bracelet."

That gave Jessie an idea. "Remember what we did *before* Mateo went to his room? We poured some of the candy into the other bags so everyone would have the same amount. Gloria, Violet, and Benny—you should check your bags too."

"Well," Benny said, "I know it's not in my bag, because I've already eaten all my candy."

"*All* of it?" Jessie said, her eyes wide.

Benny gave her a sheepish smile. "Yes. But I do happen to have Violet's candy bag. It's outside with my bike."

Now it was Violet's turn to laugh with surprise. "I told you, didn't I? Benny always eats my candy."

"Well," Henry said, "let's look inside!"

Benny ran and grabbed the bag and brought it into the backyard. He turned the bag upside down and dumped the contents out onto the grass. Among the candy bars and empty wrappers, something shiny sparkled in the sunlight.

"The bracelet!" Gloria said. She threw her arms around Benny. "You found it!" She held the bracelet in her hands, her face beaming. Mateo gave her a hug and then Tina gave him a high five. All the children were happy that the mystery was finally solved. But suddenly Gloria raised her eyebrows.

"We'd better return this soon," she said. "Mamá and Papá have already left to set up for the Day of

The Day of the Dead Mystery

the Dead celebration at Greenfield Park, and that means they took the altar with them!"

Family First

Mateo put their great-grandmother's bracelet back in the jewelry box and zipped it in the pocket of his jacket. Tina waved good-bye to the others, and they jumped onto their bikes and pedaled toward Greenfield Park. As they got close, they saw families carrying large baskets of food and colorful decorations. Many people had Catrina makeup on their faces, just like Gloria and Mateo, and it made it look like the sidewalk was fully of happy skeletons on their way to a party.

"I hope it's not too late to bring back the bracelet," Gloria yelled over her shoulder to the others, who were riding behind her. Benny noticed that she looked pretty worried.

The Day of the Dead Mystery

The bike path curved beneath a stone archway and into Greenfield Park. Along a tall fence on the west side of the park, families were setting up their altars. The sun was getting lower in the sky, with evening not too far behind. The children knew they didn't have a moment to waste.

They locked up their bikes and ran, with Gloria leading the way, until they found the Hidalgo family's altar. Mr. Hidalgo stood in front of it, and deep lines creased his forehead. He seemed to be arguing with a man the Aldens had never met.

"You should have been more careful with the bracelet," the man was saying. He sighed. "I can't believe you let this happen."

"Uncle Jorge," Gloria said to the man.

He turned to the children, and his face softened. "Hello, kids," he said. "Your dad and I were just talking about—"

"This?" Mateo asked. He pulled the jewelry box from his pocket and opened it to show his father and uncle that the bracelet had been safely returned.

Mr. Hidalgo and Uncle Jorge stood with wide eyes as Mateo explained the whole story of what had happened with the bracelet. "I should have told you sooner," Mateo said, "but I was so afraid that Great-Grandmother Luisa's spirit wouldn't make it back to visit us for Day of the Dead, and it would be all my fault."

"Mateo," said Mr. Hidalgo. He put his hand on his son's shoulder. "I'm sorry you felt that way. Even though this bracelet is worth a lot of money and is very important to our family, the objects are not as important as the memories and stories of your great-grandmother. Those can never be lost," he said with a tear in his eye. "And no one can ever take them from us."

Mr. Hidalgo pulled up one of the charms on the bracelet and turned it over so Mateo could see an inscription on the back. "*La familia es primero*," Mr. Hidalgo read. "That means 'family comes first.' Even if you had lost the bracelet for good, Mateo, your great-grandmother would not have wanted the family to be divided."

"That's right," Uncle Jorge said, looking at Mr. Hidalgo. "Your dad was there for me this year when the library lost funding for my job. And I would do

the same for him if he ever needed my help. Family comes first."

"Is that why you took the bracelet to the jewelers, Papá?" Gloria asked her father. "To see how much it was worth?"

Mr. Hidalgo sighed. "I will admit I did think about selling it, but only so that I could give the money to Jorge. But the more I thought about it, the more I realized it would make more sense to have him stay with us for good, even when he gets another job. That's what my grandmother would have wanted, for all of us to be together."

Uncle Jorge nodded. "That's what I think too, even when we argue." He smiled. "Remember when she used to say we were *como uña y mugre*? That meant we were always together...and always getting into trouble."

Mr. Hidalgo laughed. "She would say that when she found us getting into the cookies. But only because she loved to eat them so much herself and wanted to be sure we didn't take them all."

As the brothers shared their memories, Gloria glanced over at the family's altar. "This is exactly what Day of the Dead is for, isn't it?" she said. "To tell the stories and remember."

"Papá," said Mateo, "will you tell us more stories about Great-Grandmother Luisa?"

"Of course!" said Mr. Hidalgo. "But first, let's get everyone some food. Kids, would you like some tamales?"

"Yes!" Benny said, almost before Mr. Hidalgo had finished speaking.

But Jessie looked at her watch and then put her hand on Benny's arm. "We'd love to," she said, "but, actually, we have to get going." She looked at her siblings. "Remember, Grandfather told us to be home by five thirty, and it's already five fifteen!"

CHAPTER 10

Celebrate!

The Alden children put their bikes in the garage. Just as they were about to go inside, they saw Grandfather waving to them from the door of the boxcar in the backyard. Henry and Jessie looked at each other in surprise.

"I wonder what Grandfather's doing out here," Henry said.

"Let's find out," Violet said.

The children ran across the yard to join him.

"How was the party?" Grandfather asked.

"Really fun," Jessie said. "Gloria and Mateo found their great-grandmother's bracelet."

"That's good news," Grandfather said. "I knew they would."

"Their whole family seemed really happy," Benny said. "The bracelet isn't the most important thing, but having it does help them remember her and pass the memories down to the kids who were too young to know her."

"Benny, it's funny you should mention memories," Grandfather said. "Before the Hidalgos moved to our neighborhood, I never knew much about Day of the Dead. But as we have become friends, I have been lucky to learn about the ways they celebrate and remember their ancestors. It's inspired me to honor our own family memories in a new way."

Grandfather Alden opened the door to the boxcar, and the children peered inside. There was a long dining table that nearly filled the whole space, covered in a white tablecloth with enough place settings for their family. Standing beside the table was Watch and Mrs. McGregor. She had a big smile on her face.

"What's all this?" Jessie asked.

"Go on in and see for yourself," Grandfather said.

The Aldens climbed inside. Lanterns on the

table lit the space, and after the children's eyes adjusted to the light, they noticed another smaller table behind Mrs. McGregor. It too was covered in a tablecloth, and it held a row of framed photos.

"Look," Violet whispered. She touched the edge of a silver frame. "It's Mom and Dad at their wedding."

"And here they are holding you, Benny," Henry said, pointing to another photo that showed Mr. and Mrs. Alden cuddling a baby in a snowsuit. In front of the picture frame was a hammer. "What's this for?" Henry wondered.

Jessie remembered what they had learned about the objects families placed on altars in memory of their loved ones. "I think the hammer is there because Dad was a carpenter."

Grandfather nodded. "And I've included sheet music, in honor of your mother. She was a wonderful pianist," he said.

"And look," Violet whispered. She pointed at a teacup that looked a little worse for wear. It had been broken and not quite perfectly glued back together. "Mom's teacup. Do you remember what she said when I broke it? 'I can always get another teacup. I can't get another you.' That was just a little time before..." Violet couldn't quite say the words *before the accident*.

Celebrate!

Jessie and Henry looked at her with sad eyes and nodded. "And there is the spool of thread," Violet said. "The one the sheriff found in the car. These were the only two things I brought with us from the farm. Grandfather, you thought of everything." Violet carefully set the items back on the table and turned to give him a hug.

Jessie came over to them. "Thank you, Grandfather," she said. He hugged Jessie and Henry next. But Benny stayed quiet and continued to look at the pictures.

"Are you all right, Benny?" Mrs. McGregor asked.

Benny looked thoughtful. "When Mateo told us he decided to take the bracelet because he was upset that he didn't have any memories of his own with their great-grandmother, I knew what he meant." Benny's voice sounded a little shaky.

Violet reached over and squeezed his hand. "I feel the same way. Sometimes it's hard for me to remember the times our family had together before the accident—before we had to move away. Sometimes it feels like the memories are slipping away."

"I feel that way too sometimes," Henry said

softly. "But do you remember what Gloria told us the first night she showed us her family's altar?"

"Yes," Jessie said, nodding. "That Day of the Dead is a celebration of people loved and lost, and that honoring them is an important job."

"That's right," Grandfather Alden said. "And I say we begin our celebration right now."

The Aldens took their seats around the table, and Mrs. McGregor uncovered the hot serving dishes in the center. One held roast chicken with lemon slices and fragrant sprigs of rosemary. The next held broccoli and carrots, and the third dish was a steaming hot casserole full of macaroni and cheese.

Jessie smiled at Grandfather. "I'm so glad you remembered! Macaroni and cheese was Mom's favorite!"

"It was?" Benny asked. "I can't believe it. That's my favorite food too!"

"I can believe it, Benny," Grandfather Alden said. "You are like your mother in so many ways. For one thing, you have her smile."

"I do?" Benny said, then smiled and glanced at the photo of his mother on the table, wondering if his and hers really looked the same.

"Oh, yes," Grandfather said, laughing. "And, of course, your mother absolutely loved food."

"She was such a good cook," Henry said. He looked at Jessie. "Remember that time at the farmer's market when she bought out all the blueberries they had? They filled up the whole back seat of the car. She baked so many pies that we had enough to give one to every family on our road."

Jessie laughed. "Yes. It took me days to get the stains from the berries off my hands."

"When our parents died, so many people talked about how generous Mom was," Violet said. "It sounds like they were right."

"Now, your father, Ben," Grandfather said, "was a little bit more of the quiet type."

"But what a talented man," Mrs. McGregor chimed in. She reminded the Aldens that she had known their father since he was a little boy.

"From the time he was very young, your grandmother and I knew he would grow up to do something with his hands. He was always taking things apart—the toaster, a radio—just to see if he could put them back together. Your grandmother could not have been prouder of him." Grandfather closed his eyes, as if he were lost in the memory for a moment.

This gave Jessie an idea. She asked to be excused for a moment and slipped out the door of the boxcar.

"Would anyone like seconds?" Henry asked.

"Yes, please!" Benny said, passing his plate to his brother. "I'll take more of Mom's favorite."

"And what was Dad's favorite food, Mrs. McGregor?" Violet asked.

Mrs. McGregor grinned. "That's coming up next," she said. She took a brown paper bag from under her seat, opened it, and poured the contents on the tablecloth.

"Saltwater taffy!" Violet said, delighted. "Just the same as me."

Mrs. McGregor nodded. "He would have eaten it every day if he could have."

"A man with very good taste," Violet said, which caused Grandfather to laugh.

Just then, Jessie came back into the boxcar. She was holding two things behind her back.

"Grandfather," Jessie said. "I thought some things were missing from our family's altar. Is it okay with you if I add this?"

Jessie showed him a framed photograph. The children crowded around so they could see.

"Is that Grandmother?" Benny asked Grandfather Alden. The woman in the photograph was wearing a sundress and riding a bicycle with a basket tied to the handlebars. In the basket was a puppy.

Grandfather nodded. "That was the day we found Pal, the dog we had when your father was a little boy. She found him wandering in the park and never could find his owner, so we brought him home to live with us."

"That sounds like the way we found Watch!" Benny said.

"Mrs. McGregor," Jessie said, "I hope you won't mind, but I brought the prayer book you keep next to your bed. You told me once that your husband gave it to you as a gift."

Mrs. McGregor's eyes filled with tears. "That's right," she said, and wiped them away with the back of her hand. "It belonged to his mother before that, and then he gave it to me."

"Well, you are like family to us, and I think this should be on the altar too."

Mrs. McGregor nodded, and Jessie placed the new additions on the small table. Finally, the Alden family altar was complete.

"Thank you, Jessie," Grandfather said, patting her on the shoulder. "That was a very thoughtful thing to do."

Henry glanced at his watch. His mouth was still full of taffy, so he had to chew an extra moment before he could say, "It's getting late. We should get back to the party!"

The Aldens helped Mrs. McGregor carry the dishes from the table back inside the house. Then they jumped on their bikes and rode back to the park. At the corner, they saw Mrs. Hayes and Tina walking in the same direction. They were carrying a plate of food and a huge bouquet of marigolds.

Mrs. Hayes waved to the children. "Isn't this a wonderful celebration? See you at the park!"

The children waved back and rode on. The streetlights had come on, and through the windows of the houses they passed on Miller Street, Benny could see families, some large, some small, sitting together at their kitchen tables, eating and laughing and enjoying each other's company. He realized that memories weren't just something in the past. They were something families were making all the time. When Grandfather had taken the children's picture before they went trick-or-treating, that had become a memory. This right now—riding his bike with Henry, Jessie, and Violet to be with their friends for Day of the Dead—this would become a happy family memory too. The thought made Benny smile.

Back in the park, the Day of the Dead party was in full swing. Strings of lights hung in the trees, and candles flickered in the darkness, illuminating the pictures families had put up to remember loved ones. Children chased each other around the tables, giggling and swiping candy when their parents weren't looking. The adults greeted each other with hugs and handshakes.

At the Hidalgos' altar, Mrs. Hidalgo was handing out cups of soda and more of her delicious tamales.

The Day of the Dead Mystery

Great-Grandmother Luisa's picture sat behind the jewelry box with the heirloom bracelet tucked inside, finally back where it belonged.

"You're back!" Gloria said to the Aldens. "Did you enjoy your grandfather's surprise?"

"Yes!" Benny said. He told the Hidalgos about the special dinner Grandfather and Mrs. McGregor had prepared and all the memories the family had shared.

"That's wonderful," Mrs. Hidalgo said. She wore even more elaborate Catrina makeup than Gloria and Mateo—a big skeleton's grin painted around her mouth, and colorful flowers cascading down her neck and shoulders.

"Ah," Mr. Hidalgo said, pointing to the far end of the path that was strewn with bright orange marigold petals. "Here comes the music."

The children turned to see a group of musicians walking through the park. Two women strummed small guitars, and behind them one man played a larger guitar and another played a drum. The musicians began to sing in Spanish.

Gloria looked at her parents in surprise. "Isn't

this song one of Great-Grandmother's favorites?"

Mr. Hidalgo nodded and smiled. "That's right. You have a good memory, Gloria."

"Keeping memories alive is what this day is all about," Uncle Jorge added. He smiled at his brother, and the men shook hands. Then he lifted his cup. "*La familia es primero*," he said.

Mateo nodded in agreement. "The family comes first." Then he began to dance and clap along with the music. "Now, let's celebrate!"

About Day of the Dead

Día de Muertos, or Day of the Dead, is celebrated in Mexico, parts of Latin America, and some Latin American communities around the world. The two-day celebration is a time to remember those who have died, but that does not mean it is meant to be sad or scary. Instead, Day of the Dead is a time in which people honor loved ones who have died and welcome their spirits back for a night.

Day of the Dead traditions go back thousands of years. Civilizations such as the Aztec empire viewed death as another part of life—as something to be accepted and embraced. The Aztecs held a month-long celebration in honor of death. Later, colonists from Spain conquered Mexico. Many of the colonists believed in Catholicism, which has its own days for remembering the dead: All Saints Day and All Souls Day. After seizing control, the colonists moved the Aztec's late-summer celebration to the first two days of November, the dates of All Saints Day and All Souls Day. Today, the ways in which people celebrate Day of the Dead continue to change, but the main purpose for the celebration remains.

The first day of Día de Muertos, November 1, is also called *Día de los Angelitos,* or "Day of the Little Angels." It is a time to remember children and infants who have passed away. In memory of these young ones, families put toys and candy onto altars called *ofrendas.*

The second day, November 2, is the day to celebrate and honor adults who have died. On both days, people decorate ofrendas with candles and pictures. It is also common to put beverages; *pan de muerto,* or "bread of the dead"; and *caleveras de azúcar,* or "sugar skulls," onto the ofrenda.

According to one tradition, spirits of the dead travel to the land of the living during Día de

Muertos. The journey is long and exhausting, and the food, drinks, and treats are meant to help the spirits regain their strength. Some people also put out blankets and pillows so spirits can rest. *Flores de cempazuchitl*, or marigold flowers, are also common on Day of the Dead. The marigold's bright orange color and strong smell are believed to help lead souls back home.

In Mexico, many people celebrate Day of the Dead in cemeteries. People set up ofrendas, clean off grave sites, hold picnics, and spend time telling stories about loved ones who have died. In countries such as the United States, cemeteries have different rules, making it more difficult to celebrate Day of the Dead at grave sites. In addition, many recent immigrants may not have relatives in their country's cemeteries. People have adapted by keeping ofrendas in their homes or by gathering together for community celebrations in parks, churches, and cultural centers.

Community celebrations of Day of the Dead often involve face painting and dressing up like skeletons. This style of art, known as *La Catrina*, is a way of making light of death. Along with singing, dancing, and holding parades, it is another way for communities to joyfully connect with relatives and friends who are no longer living.

Read on for an exclusive
sneak preview of

THE LEGEND OF
THE HOWLING
WEREWOLF

the next
Boxcar Children mystery!

Grandfather Alden pulled his rental car onto the interstate. He looked over his left shoulder, waiting for traffic to pass. Then he sped up. "Couple more hours until we get to Mrs. Riley's house," he told his four grandchildren.

Ten-year-old Violet was in the backseat. Her pigtails bounced as she turned to see the road signs. "'Welcome to Idaho,'" she read aloud. Another sign whizzed by. "'Famous Potatoes.'"

"'Where are all the potatoes, Grandfather?" she asked.

He nodded toward the windows. "See all those bare fields out there? Desert, really. Miles and miles of crops have already been harvested. It's October, so potatoes are being sent to all parts of the country by train and truck."

"For French fries and hash browns, right, Grandfather?" six-year-old Benny, who was sitting next to Violet, said.

Grandfather smiled at Benny in his rearview mirror. "That's right," he said. "When we get to Townsend, you'll see that sugar beets are another important crop in Idaho. They're part of a fun event this weekend."

"That's exciting," said Benny. "When will we get there?"

"Soon," said Grandfather for the fifth time that hour. "Try to enjoy the view, Benny. Do you know those mountains in the distance?"

"Uh, no, not really," Benny said. He looked to his brother in the front seat for an answer.

"Those are the Rockies," said fourteen-year-old Henry. "They go all the way from Canada down to New Mexico. They'll be covered with snow all winter."

After a while, they passed some hills with steep sides and flat tops.

"They look like tables," said Jessie.

"Those are called buttes," Grandfather explained. "They are actually volcanic cones. See their black sides?"

"Lava!" said Henry. "We studied buttes in science

class. Volcanoes used to bubble up here. And when the lava dried, it made the buttes. But I think these volcanoes have been sleeping for a long time."

"That's right, Henry," said Grandfather.

"What if they wake up while we're here?" asked Violet.

"The last eruption was about two thousand years ago," Grandfather said. "No need to worry. And here we are." He slowed the car, clicked on his turn signal, and took the exit.

"Look, Benny, we're almost there," said Henry. He pointed to a sign out the window.

"'Welcome to Townsend. Home of the Sage Hen,'" Benny read slowly. "What's that mean, Grandfather?"

"It looks like a chicken," said Violet, who was looking at the bird shown on the sign.

"It does, I suppose," Grandfather said with a chuckle. "Sage hens are also called sage grouse. Strange creatures. The males do this funny dance to attract the females. It's quite the sight. That's one reason a lot of tourists come up to places like Townsend."

"I hope we can get a close look," said Jessie. "And I want to see some lava." She was twelve, and she loved animals. She rolled down the window for her dog, Watch, so he could sniff the cool autumn air.

"I hope we see them too," said Henry. As the oldest, he liked to take charge. "Maybe I can lead us all on a hike. And hopefully we'll come across an old volcano."

"You'll have plenty of time to explore in the next few days," said Grandfather. "When I was a boy, I went to summer camp here. The area is rich in geology and Native American history."

As Grandfather drove down Main Street, he said, "I'm excited for you to meet my friend Mrs. Riley. She has a big project I think will interest you all."

"I can't wait to meet her," said Jessie.

Violet looked over at her grandfather. "We love projects!"

"Yes, I know, dear." Grandfather gave her a friendly wink.

The Alden children were orphans. After their parents died, they had learned they must go live with a grandfather they had never met. They heard he was mean, so they ran away to the woods, where they found shelter in an old boxcar. That's where they found their wire fox terrier, Watch. Soon their grandfather found them. He wasn't mean at all! He brought them to his home in Greenfield, Connecticut, to live as a family. He even had the boxcar brought to his backyard. Now the Aldens used it as their clubhouse.

Grandfather traveled often. When possible, he brought his grandchildren with him so they would have new experiences. This trip had brought him to Boise, Idaho. And now he and the children were on their way across the state to visit his friend Mrs. Riley.

***

Trees along Townsend's Main Street were gold and crimson with fall leaves. Grandfather turned up a gravel driveway just outside of town. A single-story ranch house sat in a field of sagebrush. Wide windows faced the foothills of the mountains.

A woman in jeans and a plaid shirt came from the front porch to greet the Aldens. Her long dark hair hung in a braid over her shoulder. She wore turquoise earrings and a turquoise bracelet. She shook hands with Grandfather and smiled at the children. "I'm Susan Riley," she told them. "I'm very happy to meet you. And, James, it's wonderful to see you again."

"Thank you for inviting us, Susan," said Grandfather.

She turned to the children. "This is a good weekend to be here because it's our very first Harvest Festival. I'm on the City Council and am one of the festival organizers."

"That sounds like fun," said Jessie. "Do you need any help?"

"Actually, yes," the woman said. "There is much to do, and it would be nice to have some help. Would that interest you?"

"Yes!" Violet replied quickly.

"I love to help," Benny said.

"We all do," Jessie said. "The middle school Henry and I go to will give us extra credit for community service. But even if they didn't, we would still want to help you."

"That's right," Henry agreed.

"Well come on in," Mrs. Riley said. "I've set out some snacks in case anyone's hungry."

Benny's face lit up. His family laughed. "Benny's always hungry," Jessie explained.

"Then you're in the right place," their hostess said. She waved them inside, and they went to the kitchen. A table in the center of the room had plates of sliced apples, cheese, and crackers. "Sit, please," she said, pouring each child a glass of milk. She brought Grandfather a steaming mug of tea. Watch curled up under the table, waiting for any dropped food.

"What is the Harvest Festival?" Benny asked. "Is it for the potatoes your town planted?"

"Good question, Benny," the woman replied. "Idaho certainly is famous for potatoes, but the big crop around Townsend is sugar beets."

"Sugar beets?" Jessie said. "Do people make a pie or cake with those?"

"In a way, yes," Mrs. Riley said. "But first the beets are sent to factories. They're processed into the type of sugar used for baking. Soda companies also use it to sweeten soft drinks."

"But can you eat a sugar beet like one of these apples?" Benny asked.

Mrs. Riley laughed. "I'll let you find out tomorrow, Benny. Meanwhile, I'll show you all to where you are staying so you can settle in."

When the children were done eating, they took their plates to the sink. Then they went and got their bags from the car. After picking where they would sleep, they joined Grandfather and Mrs. Riley on the back deck. She was looking at the foothills, now golden in the afternoon sun.

"Are there any sage grouse out there?" Henry asked.

"Probably," she replied. "Not only are they becoming rare, but they're hard to spot. Their feathers are camouflaged in the brush."

Jessie opened her notebook and clicked her pen. "Mrs. Riley, what do you need help with to get ready for the Harvest Festival? Just tell us, and we'll get started."

"That's very kind, Jessie. Thank you." Mrs. Riley continued to stare at the hills. "Something's been troubling me though."

"What is it, Susan?" Grandfather asked.

She sighed. "I'm worried no one will show up on Sunday. Especially for the evening parade."

"Why is that?" asked Henry.

"For the past few months, a rumor has been going around town," Mrs. Riley said. "A strange and upsetting rumor."

The Alden children exchanged glances. They looked at their host with concern.

"What rumor?" Violet asked. She suddenly felt cold and rubbed her arms to warm up.

Mrs. Riley motioned toward the foothills. "Someone posted on our website that a werewolf lives up there," she said.

Benny gulped. He said, "A werewolf?"

Mrs. Riley nodded. "Yes," she said. "And when the harvest moon gets full, as it will this weekend, the creature supposedly sneaks into town. Some people are afraid of going outside."

The children were quiet for a moment. Then Henry said, "But there's no such thing as a werewolf. Isn't that right, Grandfather?"

"I'm certain they don't exist," said Grandfather.

Violet looked up at Grandfather. In a quiet voice she said, "But what if they do exist?"

Introducing The Boxcar Children Early Readers!

Adapted from the beloved chapter books, these new early readers allow kids to begin reading with the stories that started it all. Look for *The Yellow House Mystery* and *Mystery Ranch,* coming Spring 2019!

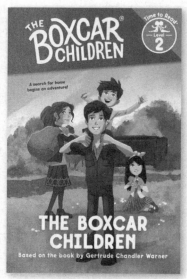

978-0-8075-0839-8 · US $12.99

978-0-8075-7675-5 · US $12.99

Add to Your
Boxcar Children Collection
with New Books and Sets!

The first twelve books are now available in
three individual boxed sets!

978-0-8075-0854-1 · US $24.99   978-0-8075-0857-2 · US $24.99   978-0-8075-0840-4 · US $24.99

The Boxcar Children Bookshelf includes the first twelve
books, a bookmark with complete title checklist,
and a poster with activities.

978-0-8075-0855-8 · US $69.99

The Boxcar Children 20-Book Set includes Gertrude
Chandler Warner's original nineteen books,
plus an all-new activity book, stickers,
and a magnifying glass!

978-0-8075-0847-3 · US $132.81

978-0-8075-2850-1 · US $6.99

Introducing Interactive Mysteries!

Have you ever wanted to help the Aldens crack a case? Now you can with this interactive, choose-your-path-style mystery!

The Boxcar Children, Fully Illustrated!

This fully illustrated edition celebrates Gertrude Chandler Warner's timeless story. Featuring all-new full-color artwork as well as an afterword about the author, the history of the book, and the Boxcar Children legacy, this volume will be treasured by first-time readers and longtime fans alike.

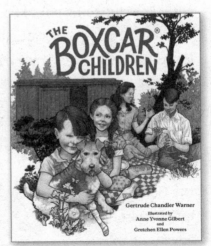

978-0-8075-0925-8 · US $34.99

THE BOXCAR CHILDREN

GREAT ADVENTURE

An Exciting 5-Book Miniseries

**Henry, Jessie, Violet, and Benny Alden
are on a secret mission that takes
them around the world!**

When Violet finds a turtle statue that nobody's seen
before in an old trunk at home, the children are on the
case! The clue turns out to be an invitation to the
Reddimus Society, a secret guild dedicated to returning
lost treasures to where they belong.

Now the Aldens must take the statue and six mysterious
boxes across the country to deliver them safely—and keep
them out of the hands of the Reddimus Society's enemies.
It's just the beginning of
the Boxcar Children's
most amazing
adventure yet!

HC 978-0-8075-0695-0
PB 978-0-8075-0696-7

HC 978-0-8075-0698-1
PB 978-0-8075-0699-8

HC 978-0-8075-0684-4
PB 978-0-8075-0685-1

HC 978-0-8075-0687-5
PB 978-0-8075-0688-2

HC 978-0-8075-0681-3
PB 978-0-8075-0682-0

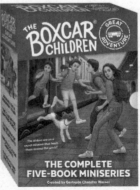

Also available as a boxed set!
978-0-8075-0693-6 • $34.95

Hardcover US $12.99 • Paperback US $6.99

GERTRUDE CHANDLER WARNER discovered when she was teaching that many readers who like an exciting story could find no books that were both easy and fun to read. She decided to try to meet this need, and her first book, *The Boxcar Children*, quickly proved she had succeeded.

Miss Warner drew on her own experiences to write the mystery. As a child she spent hours watching trains go by on the tracks opposite her family home. She often dreamed about what it would be like to set up housekeeping in a caboose or freight car—the situation the Alden children find themselves in.

While the mystery element is central to each of Miss Warner's books, she never thought of them as strictly juvenile mysteries. She liked to stress the Aldens' independence and resourcefulness and their solid New England devotion to using up and making do. The Aldens go about most of their adventures with as little adult supervision as possible—something else that delights young readers.

Miss Warner lived in Putnam, Connecticut, until her death in 1979. During her lifetime, she received hundreds of letters from girls and boys telling her how much they liked her books.